Jacques' Jungle Ballet

Written by Karen Lavut   Illustrated by Nicola Rigg

Henry Holt and Company
New York

Once upon a time there was a young
elephant who lived in the jungle with his
family and all the other wild animals.
His name was Jacques. Jacques enjoyed
clomping through the forest with his
brothers and sisters, pulling leaves off the
trees to eat, spraying himself in the pond
and resting in the shade at midday. But
he was not completely satisfied.

Jacques wanted to be a ballet dancer.

His parents were baffled. They had no idea how Jacques could ever have seen, or even heard of, the ballet. They told him to get that silly idea right out of his head. They told him that elephants were meant to be elephants, not dancers.

"I won't have a son of mine turning into a ballet dancer!" shouted his father angrily.

"He'll grow out of it, dear," said his mother soothingly.

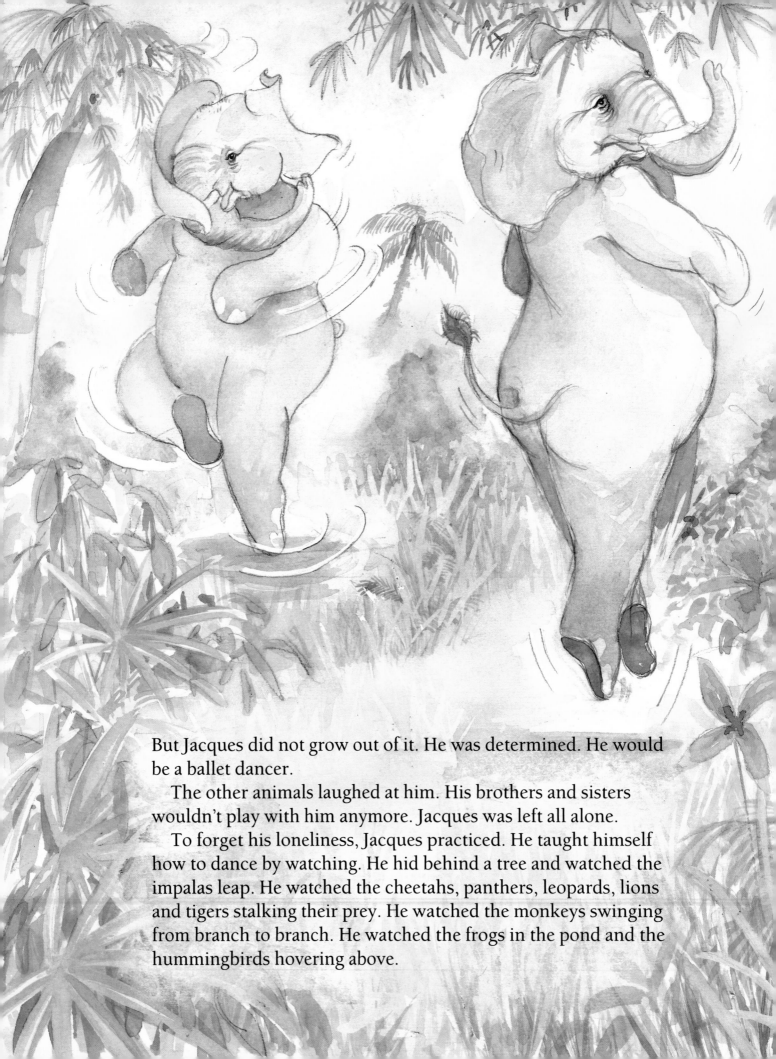

But Jacques did not grow out of it. He was determined. He would be a ballet dancer.

The other animals laughed at him. His brothers and sisters wouldn't play with him anymore. Jacques was left all alone.

To forget his loneliness, Jacques practiced. He taught himself how to dance by watching. He hid behind a tree and watched the impalas leap. He watched the cheetahs, panthers, leopards, lions and tigers stalking their prey. He watched the monkeys swinging from branch to branch. He watched the frogs in the pond and the hummingbirds hovering above.

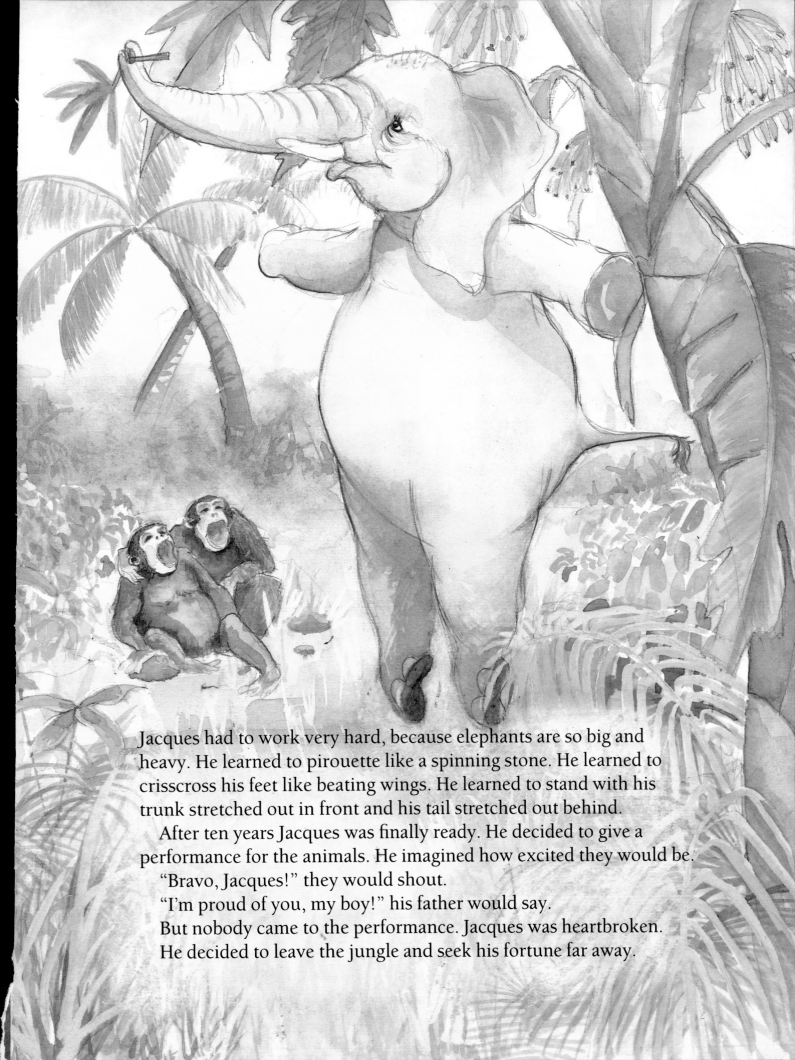

Jacques had to work very hard, because elephants are so big and heavy. He learned to pirouette like a spinning stone. He learned to crisscross his feet like beating wings. He learned to stand with his trunk stretched out in front and his tail stretched out behind.

After ten years Jacques was finally ready. He decided to give a performance for the animals. He imagined how excited they would be.

"Bravo, Jacques!" they would shout.

"I'm proud of you, my boy!" his father would say.

But nobody came to the performance. Jacques was heartbroken.

He decided to leave the jungle and seek his fortune far away.

Jacques walked for three days, until his path was blocked by a river. The river was full of crocodiles. But Jacques swam across. Every time a crocodile came near him, he gave a terrific kick. His legs were very strong from his training.

He walked and walked until there were no more trees and no more grass — only sand. He nearly died of thirst. But he staggered on, until at last he came to a mountain.

Slowly and painfully Jacques climbed the mountain. When he got to the top, he could see a city.

"There are thousands of people in a city!" said Jacques to himself. "They'll know all about ballet. They'll understand why I want to dance!"

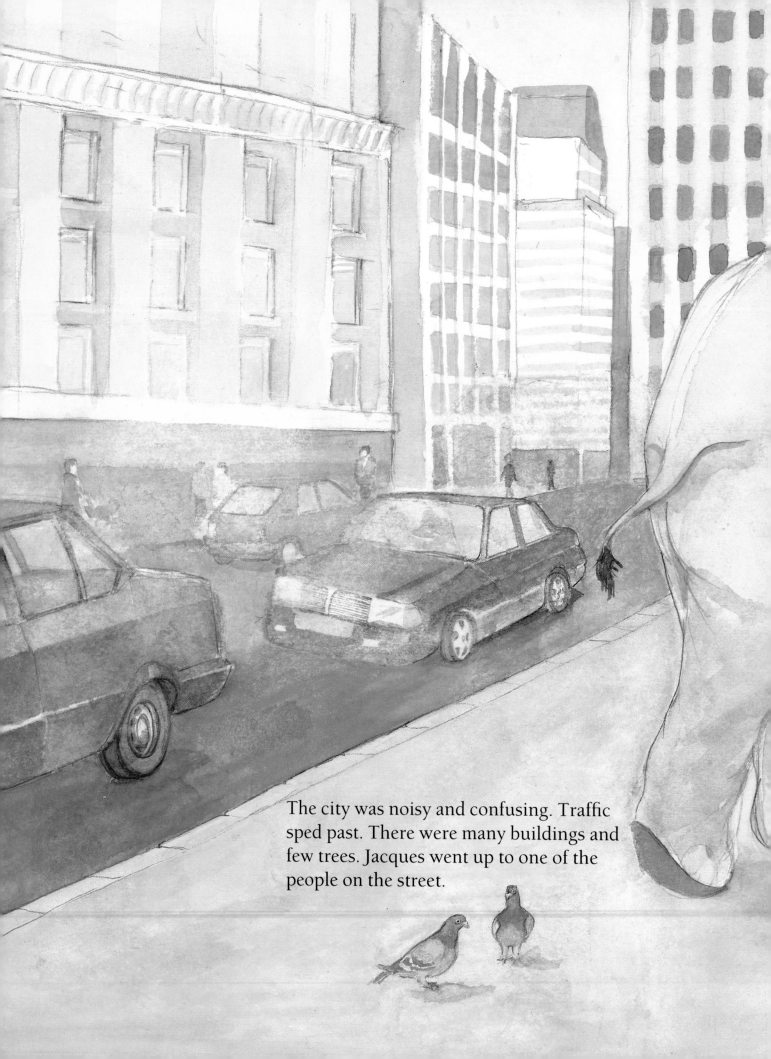

The city was noisy and confusing. Traffic sped past. There were many buildings and few trees. Jacques went up to one of the people on the street.

"Excuse me, is there a ballet company in this city?"

The stranger noticed that Jacques was an elephant, but being polite, she did not comment. She took him to the Ballet Theater. Jacques thanked her with a bow.

Jacques knocked on the stage door. It was opened by the manager, who said rudely, "What do you want?"

"Good morning, sir. I'm a ballet dancer. I would like to dance with your company," said Jacques.

"You're not a ballet dancer — you're an elephant! Get out!"

And he slammed the door in Jacques' face.

The next morning Jacques was back.

"You again!" said the manager.

"I may be an elephant, but I'm also a dancer," said Jacques.

"Out! Out! Out!" screamed the manager so loudly that the director came rushing to the door. He was surprised to find the manager shouting at an elephant.

"What's going on here?" he asked. The director's name was Basil. He smiled at Jacques and said, "What can I do for you?"

"Please let me dance in your company," said Jacques.

"But you're an elephant—"

"I'm a dancer! I'm good, I'm really good!"

"That doesn't matter — you're still an elephant. Elephants are very nice — they aren't meant for the stage, that's all. You're too big and heavy."

Jacques sank his head onto his chest. A tear trickled down his cheek.

Basil didn't know what to do. He felt sorry for Jacques, but he was in the middle of a dress rehearsal. "Here's a free ticket for tonight's show. I'm sure you'll enjoy it. Good-bye, now, and good luck."

That evening, hundreds of people were standing outside the theater, waiting to buy tickets. Jacques handed his ticket to an usher. "I'm sorry, sir, but you're too big for the seat. Would you mind standing at the back?"

He had an excellent view. The place was as crowded as the jungle. The audience was talking softly, not like the chattering and shrieking he was used to. There was a delicate smell of perfume — not as strong as the jungle smell of earth and flowers. Then he heard the orchestra tuning up — that sounded like the jungle!

The lights dimmed slowly until it was dark. There was quiet. A spotlight shone on a man who bowed, then faced the orchestra and raised his hands. He was the conductor! And then there was the most wonderful music Jacques had ever heard.

Slowly the curtain rose.

When the ballet was over, the audience applauded wildly and threw flowers onto the stage. But Jacques couldn't move. He was spellbound. Tears of joy stood in his eyes.

Jacques was at the ballet again the next night. And the next. He came every night for a whole week.

At the end of the week Jacques was at the stage door again.

"Oh dear," sighed Basil.

Without wasting another word, Jacques did a pirouette and an arabesque.

"Extraordinary!" gasped Basil. "But you're the wrong shape. I'm terribly sorry. Why don't you try the circus?"

So that's what Jacques did.

He found the circus tent in a big park. "Excuse me!" he called.

A woman came out of the tent. Her name was Monica, and she was the owner. "Yes?" she snapped.

"Good afternoon, madam. I am a ballet dancer, and —"

"A ballet dancer? Don't make me laugh! It takes a year to get a brute like you to stand on two legs — much less dance! Ha, ha! Tell me another!"

Jacques was learning fast that words were useless. He made a running leap and did a triple turn in the air.

"Well, well, well!" said Monica. "Why didn't you say so? I think we can use you — when can you start?"

"Right now," said Jacques.

That evening Jacques saw hundreds of people filing into the big top. He heard a band playing. He saw animals being led into the tent, and clowns running behind them. Then came the jugglers, acrobats and trapeze artists.

At long last Monica came for Jacques. "You need dressing up." She tied a red-velvet sash around Jacques' waist and a bunch of purple feathers behind each ear. Then she led Jacques to the entrance. "Now's your big moment," she said. "You'd better be good. Ladies and gentlemen! We are proud to present the greatest ballet dancer on earth — Jacques, the elephant!"

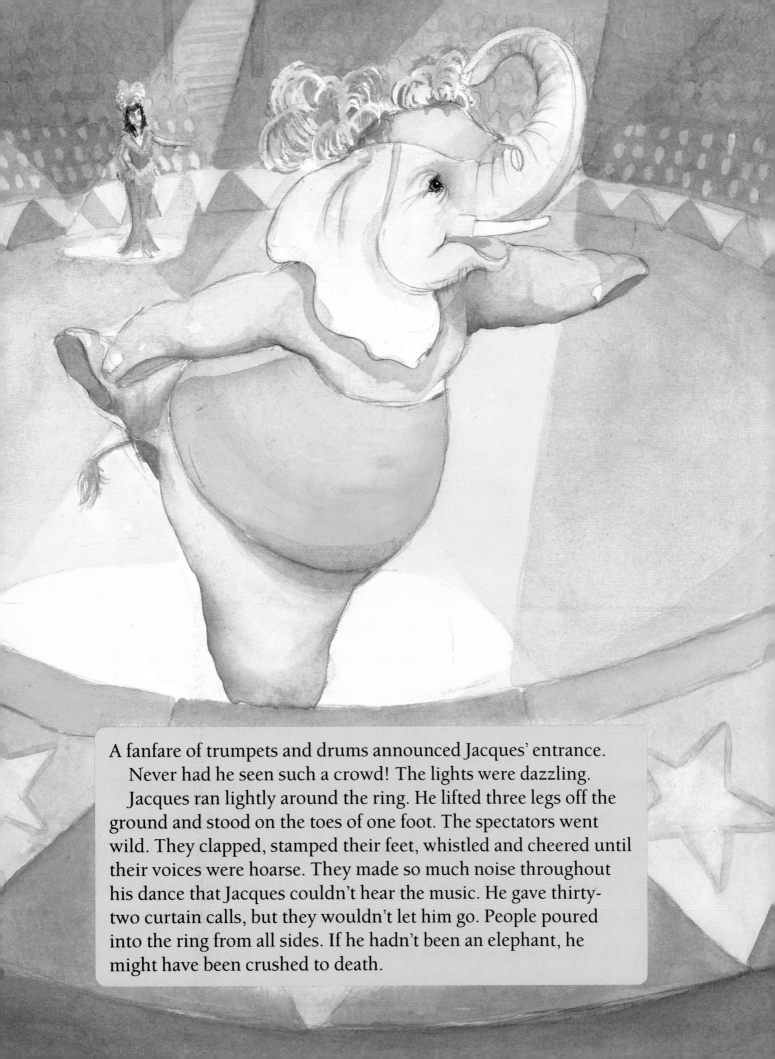

A fanfare of trumpets and drums announced Jacques' entrance.
Never had he seen such a crowd! The lights were dazzling.
Jacques ran lightly around the ring. He lifted three legs off the
ground and stood on the toes of one foot. The spectators went
wild. They clapped, stamped their feet, whistled and cheered until
their voices were hoarse. They made so much noise throughout
his dance that Jacques couldn't hear the music. He gave thirty-
two curtain calls, but they wouldn't let him go. People poured
into the ring from all sides. If he hadn't been an elephant, he
might have been crushed to death.

Jacques became famous overnight. Tons of flowers were delivered to him. People flocked to see him. He was written about in the newspapers and talked about on the radio. He was on television. A red carpet was laid from his trailer to the big top. Hundreds of people were turned away from his shows. Monica became a millionaire.

But Jacques wasn't happy.

The crowds gave him no privacy. They followed him everywhere. He longed for a quiet place to hide in peace. But Monica wouldn't let Jacques out of her sight.

Jacques didn't even enjoy doing his act. The loud music hurt his ears. It sounded ugly after the beautiful ballet music. The silly feathers and ridiculous sashes he had to wear embarrassed him. Monica made him perform sensational feats all the time. Jacques didn't want to show off in stupid costumes to flashy music. He wanted to dance — gracefully, superbly, sublimely — like a real ballet dancer.

He decided to leave the circus.